Poems
from the
Circle of Seven

A sampler to savor

IMPORTANT NOTICES

Copyright © 2023 Poems from the Circle of Seven

All rights reserved by individual authors: Nancy Cathers Demme, elliot m rubin, Virginia Watts, William Waldorf, Rodney Richards, Anne Miller Christensen, and Joan Menapace

No part of this publication may be reproduced, distributed, or transmitted in any form or by any means, including photocopying and recording, or other electronic or mechanical methods, without the prior written permission of the author, except in brief quotations embodied in reviews and certain non-commercial uses permitted by copyright law. For permission requests, contact the publisher who will forward it to the respective author(s)

ISBN 979-8986360324

Library of Congress LCCN 2023901714

Edited by Rodney Richards
Cover design and Co7 spot art by Joan Menapace

Photos or images chosen and owned or licensed for commercial use by their respective authors or from the public domain

First edition

ABLiA Media LLC, Publisher, Hamilton NJ USA
Email 1950ablia@gmail.com

Disclaimer

All sentiments expressed may contain views, facts, fiction, observations, wishes, musings, dreams, even whimsy, as presented by their respective authors

Contents

Preface i
Nancy Cathers Demme 1
   Baggage 1
   Facts of Life 3
   Clasping Water 4
   Thigh-High in Meadow Grass 5
   Mr. Blessing 6
   Grey Tears 9
elliot m rubin 10
   the closet poet 10
   lilliputian bakery 11
   on the bard 12
   that bug 13
   schoolhouse slaughterhouse 14
   viewpoint at 76 15
   false marketing 16
   america 2022 17
   arcade games 18
   adrift in poetry 19
Virginia Watts 20
   Mountain Cousins 20
   Brides 22
   In the ER with my Father 24
   The Carlisle Indian Industrial School, Pennsylvania 26
   Someone Was Always Coughing in Donora 28
   Keepsakes 30
   Capsized 31
   War Crimes 32

William Waldorf 34
Changeling 34
War Souvenirs... 35
flowers for the trip 36
Green monsters 37
Mahsa Amini.. 38
for eternity... 39
A Nude descends 40
craft room voices... 41
Mona Lisa thoughts 42
Dust in the wind 43

Rodney Richards 44
for the factory's cheesecake 44
Cardinal Rules for Mates 45
the stage 46
Can humans be fixed? 47
24/7 restaurants 48
she spoke to me... 49
silver dollar senyru 50
unbidden.. 51
on the city street at night.. 52
street kid polyglot 53

Anne Miller Christensen... 54
I Rock.. 54
One... 54
First Light 55
The Church of Poetry 55
Battle lines 56
The Sacred Space 57
Waxed Amaryllis... 57

Psalm 151	58
Embroidery in the time of pandemic	59
Awake	59
With Utter Joy	60
Poem of Recommendation	61
The Book Club	62
My Dream	63
Joan Menapace	64
Red Wagon	64
Allie	66
jubilation	67
Over-stimulated	68
Preparations	69
out walking: thoughts	70
the blue hour	71
The Mist & the Meadow	72
The Perennial Quarrel	73
Inspired by Grace Paley's poem, *I Went Out Walking*	75
Poet Bios	77
In closing . . .	81

Preface

The Circle of Seven (Co7) is a poetry trading post that religiously meets on Sundays. Our bonds, fueled by Zoom and forged under pandemic conditions, continue to ignite inspiration.

Co7 members are geographically diverse and united in generous supportive and constructive feedback. Laughs are heard in the process as our craft and friendships mature.

With gratitude to each other and you, curious reader, we invite you to savor 68 delicious nutritious fruits of our collective communing.

Nancy Cathers Demme

Baggage

he'd bought his ticket on the train
banging knees
down the aisle
with all his baggage

thud
sorry. sorry.
sorry.

even though he swore
he would travel light
his nose runny from
the stale air and b.o.
he took the seat by the
smeary window
his seat, with its incisions,
repaired with black duct tape
he sat and pressed his luggage
between his knees,
the lady next to him knitting,
the fellow across buried in the news
old hands at this.
he listened to the cell phone
chatter around him worried
the other passengers would all
get brain cancer

no, we won't be staying...could you...
...after all Georgia, you promised...
... No, I'd die if you...

he was in his glory
just another old man
on the train.
he rested his head on the head rest
the train accelerating

Nancy Cathers Demme

the voices dulled
the motion dreamy
surrounded by his surreal friends
the woman knitting
held up the red yarn,
my first grandchild, a boy, she said to
no one in particular.
the man across from her
rattled his paper.
he nodded even though he had promised himself
he would travel light.
a scarf, she said.

Nancy Cathers Demme

Facts of Life

I learned the facts of life
in the dusty chicken barn
climbing to the empty second story
I was filled with dread
we had planned this for weeks

our eyes never met
as we stood side by side
looking out
the feather dusted window
the meshed chicken wire
embedded
in the glass
as if chickens could
could break through

roosts cobwebbed
empty now
abandoned in soup pots and stove
while pigeons cooed from the rafters

I spied the cow outside
standing beside the blind horse
in the barb wired field
when she began her litany of what was to come
handed down
from her older sister.
her hands shaking
and silhouetted,
she calmed them
her palms flat on the glass
we were horrified, of course,
expected to be,
until the chickens below,
the survivors
of laying eggs,
brucked and clucked
and we spilled
into endless mirthful laughter
muffled by the lost feathers.

Clasping Water

like clasping water
clouds reign over the forest
ferns thrive with faint sun

like clasping water
shadows walk in bright sundown
sad beneath our feet

like clasping water
slow winds lift the lace curtains
an old woman sighs

like clasping water
the sweet poem's song flees
sparrows *fwitt* retreat

Nancy Cathers Demme

Thigh-High in Meadow Grass

he walked the Kentucky Redbone
a squirrely hound
a burly man
built the stall for the goat
a hutch for the rabbit
dog run and pen.
took the dog on forays
around the farm's perimeter
kicking up pheasant
harvested hay
built kitchen cabinets
fixed the toilet
he made decisions.

left his woman
to see to his dying
cells multiplying exponentially.
in the end
he was deprived of reason
30 miles from home
pets the invisible dog
who sits by his side
told his visitors
tomorrow,
we will walk home.

Mr. Blessing

he entered as we did,
single file
      the forward motion
shivering the white plastic skeleton
      hanging in the corner
next to the poster
      of a staring diagrammed eyeball,
the room dimmed
by low hovering clouds
      as he hung his herringbone jacket
on the clothes tree behind his desk,

a Clark Kent,
      Superman's alter ego
horn-rimmed glasses
black tie
dusty flatfoot shoes.

he placed his armful of
papers on the desk
      scattered brained
a messy pile
I sit in the second seat from the front
      near the door
the smell of floor cleaner
and the grazing field of cows
outside
      for daydreamers.

What is biology? Anyone?
the room is loud with silence.
      he calls roll.

Larry Toomer?
      Here.
Sally Van Zandt?
      Here.
Josh MacKenzie?   *Here?*

Here.

when he calls my name
he stops and looks up
    Scott's sister?
Yes. Here. I'm here

What is biology?
    I raise my hand.
Is it like how I know I'm near my grandmothers' house
by the way the air smells?
    he walks over to my desk
motions me to follow him
to the back of the room
    I'm trying to remember
what I did wrong.

on the counter are a series
    of microscopes
he removes some slides
from a tray, inserts one,
    and whispers, *Watch.*
he does this quickly
I notice his wrinkled fingers.

the classroom becomes
    a distant beehive.
his eye looks into the scope.
steps back and motions me to look.
    Onion cells. Go on. Look.
it is a miracle,
a wall of little bricks, dots in the center.

he leaves me there. he nods.
    goes back to class and calls the last few names.
I fiddle with knobs and back again.
    place the other slides back into the tray
Here.
Tomorrow we will all experiment with the microscopes.
June will bring some pond water and we will all take a look.

he says it as if he knows I've
        waded in the pond behind my house
even though it is riddled with snapping turtles.
        like the time driving with my family
on Mercer Street seeing Einstein
with his unruly white hair and sneakers.

I look around the room
        but I don't see a telephone booth
where Mr. Blessing can change.

Grey Tears

She hadn't expected the steaming, steeping corned beef
Settled in peppercorns and cardamom
Bay and dill, mace and mustard seed
Dominoed in jars on the table, the untouched meal

Believing she had spared her beautiful children
Sending them to swim with strangers, sailing the river
To laugh in leaf strewn shadows
She placed her cheek on the cool oven door

It took a summer to open, for the gas to spill
A wave of dead things crossed her mind
The bird in the alley, the ocher petals
The years vacant, stung with gravity,

The children laughed beyond reach
Tangled in the forest,
Feet skittering off the path
Sumac, the ivy poisoned, thorns

She would yell if she could
But the sweet fumed cloud languished
The children close to home
How they loved a story with a witch.

elliot m rubin

the closet poet

finally, the pronoun hive
buzzed on a pink, felt-covered, wire-hanger
was too much to bear,
the poet came out of the closet

the decision had to be made
choices: she/he, him/her, them/their, or we/us,
and what is a husband/wife called?
maybe just a lover or spouse?

and what do you call your muse,
besides every day?

elliott m rubin

lilliputian bakery

there's a bakery at the corner
they only make very small pies
but not in too many flavors,
yet just enough
to have you stand there,
waiting   to   decide
as you inhale oven-fresh smells
of apple, cherry, or lemon-lime with berries–
and they sell them in boxes of four
to challenge you on your way out the door

elliott m rubin

on the bard

that damn spot keeps popping up
seems i can't wash it out
shakespeare made it permanent
to survive scrubs and suds
but his twists have such an effect
the words play and dance on my tongue
and rattle around

it seems forever

no matter how a poet tries
not many can write in his path
or with words cut with a sword
thrust deep into plots to linger long

elliott m rubin

that bug

sits motionless
for two days
on my outside
rear screen door–
watches me
as i look back
wondering
why it never flew away

huge mosquitos
need blood
i have no intention
of feeding it
though i think
it has eyes on me
as i sit writing at my desk
next to the glass door

perhaps a spider
will have its meal today
although
i see no silken web
or maybe
it will tire of waiting
and fly away
to a neighbor's home–
i think they a juicier sip than i

elliott m rubin

schoolhouse slaughterhouse

how do you tell a parent
a child died, and
they can't swim
together anymore
in the current

a river keeps running
downstream
     at times,
         it washes away life

how can parents go upstream
when their passion to live
suddenly evaporates

their muscles weakened
their heart broken
the river will carry them
as the constant flow
never ceases

viewpoint at 76

where did the nineteen fifties go
my youth flew past, fast,
now i have snow by my ears
and barren ground on top
the speed of youth is gone
sports cars are a memory
canes and walkers stand ready
as are doctor types which end in "gist"

old ladies don't look too old now
young ones have no appeal
    why chance hurting myself–
now is my future,
the past a memory to tell of

false marketing

not every peach at the market
is unblemished
apples can have soft spots too
    if you look for them
but commercials are always perfect
good-looking people
even tall or short
or heavy set
never are there
ugly faces
with bad teeth or blemishes
shown –
would be nice
if everyone could live
in those ads

elliott m rubin

america 2022

i don't understand how i grew up pledging allegiance
to american flags every day in school for twelve years

and believed my country was unique and special
with liberty and justice for all,

while the red states had to have a different pledge;
instead of reading our constitution and its preamble

to life, liberty, and the pursuit of happiness; some sought
mistresses and became family value charlatans

 to force their religious beliefs on everyone else; it's their pursuit
of happiness, not mine or yours

and their politicians can make personal medical decisions for
everyone, and legislatures can overturn

popular votes, so elections have no meaning if we don't vote
for them– guess i'll use our flag to wipe away tears

in memory of the brave war dead who fought to make the pledge
have meaning and value in our lives

elliott m rubin

arcade games

everyone loves
the sideshow games
toss a ring,
throw a dart,
shoot a plate,
until legally purchased
military-style guns
are used on innocent civilian targets
at parades,
in supermarkets,
attending a concert,
at a bar,
then paid-for politicians
of the gun lobby
offer thoughts and prayers
for the victim's health–
yes, america has become
an arcade game

elliott m rubin

adrift in poetry

she is my pusher–
it's like a withdrawal
from strong drug addiction,
not with shakes and fever

her insight
into my stanzas
was on the mark
i now have no
sounding board
to bounce off
to see if my words,
thoughts, sequences,
make sense

poets are like sailors
caught in the middle of the ocean
in a row boat
paddled
too far from shore–
need an editor
to reel them back
into safe harbor
to make sense of their thoughts

Virginia Watts

Mountain Cousins

and I swam in an elbow
of Loyalsock Creek
during my summer visits.
My thirteenth August
the coffee-and-cream water
dyed my white bikini
brown as a twig. The suit,
too skimpy anyway.
The next summer
I didn't want aunts and uncles
thinking my suburban life
of concrete pools, tennis courts,
umpteen tv stations and malls
had already corrupted me. I wore
shorts and a Reese's Cup t-shirt.

Making braids on towels
spread over creekbank
my cousin Linda poked me,
pointed to a tourist
bragging about capturing
a salamander. When the boy
realized his palms were full
of orange poop he yelped,
dropped the poor creature.
Our cousin bellies shook,
quietly, so the boy didn't notice.
Unkind edges didn't exist
in that land of tumbling stream.
Only smooth pebbles speckled
as bird eggs, some striped
pink, red, and even gold.

Virginia Watts

I daydream of growing up again
where my ancestors founded
Elkland Friends Meetinghouse in 1872,
cleared rugged land and farmed,
where I was worthy by definition
and no one cared if I dressed like Tiegs
or played tennis like Evert.
I tell myself now
that I could have been one of them
anytime I wanted.

Virginia Watts

Brides

Afternoon sun bakes
freshly laid manure
as my school friend and I
scale pasture fence
leap cow patties smothered
with flies on the way
to her house.
No way to drive to it.
No mailbox.
No front steps.
No curtains.
A water pump.
An outhouse
with a peeling door.
A rusty trailer
dumped in a back meadow
usually for men
who harvest and leave.

Inside, twin sisters
run around
in pink Huggies.
No frig.
No tv.
Lawn chairs for furniture.
We kids sit on a worn rag rug
and share a bucket
of Kentucky Fried Chicken.
A treat just for birthdays
my friend whispers. It's not
her birthday or mine.
I make sure I eat everything,
even the parts I can't chew. Suck on
bones like she does. We wash up
in a Cool Whip container
of cold water in the sink.

Virginia Watts

I brought my Barbie
and some outfits. My friend
is afraid she will rip
the lace wedding gown.
Her Barbie looks like the one
my cousin Tammy played with.
Tammy is married now.
I transform her ratty Barbie
into a beautiful bride
with my gown. One twin
drops her drumstick
snatches the doll
and waves her over her head
between greasy fingers.
Cock-a-doodle-doo!
The mother yells
raises her hand
to slap the little one.
A distant tractor
rumbles to life. We play
with naked dolls now.
The twins really need
a diaper change. The gown
washed in pump water
dries stiff. At home
my mother's bleach fails.
That gown stinks forever.
Chicken bride.

Virginia Watts

In the ER with my Father

I watch his lips lie
No, I didn't fall. I never fall
Lips that have always been
on the thin side but now
they are barely there
imploding along with
the rest of him
shoulders unrecognizable
neck so scrawny
I imagine buried chicken bones

That's when an old woman's
bluish hand drops
from white-sheeted gurney
in the corridor
swings once
before hanging limp
silver charm bracelet
cloudy diamond
pale pink nail polish

Hand that gripped monkey bars
a boyfriend's hand
scrubbed parquet floors
changed bawling babies
clapped at dance recitals
gardened
water colored
played parchesi
pressed the remote
hand like the trembling hands
in church pews
I remember as a child
gripping rosary beads
prettier than jeweled necklaces

Virginia Watts

When the doctor asks me
Did Dad fall?
my father cups
broad hands
around his mouth
and *boo's* the same way
he put lousy baseball umpires
in their place
Tentative *booing*
erupts from another room
and then another and soon
the whole place is in an uproar
My father grins again
like a schoolboy

Virginia Watts

The Carlisle Indian Industrial School, Pennsylvania

The U.S. government is digging up the remains of dead children
whose birth names sound like the wind named them or a corn
moon
or an eagle banking over a clear night birth or the magic of a
mother.
Children with soft, puffing mouths. Bright, curious eyes.
Wrenched from loving arms. Born with no reason not to trust.

Blue Tomahawk.

Little Hawk.

Braids lopped off, bodies uniformed, languages silenced.
Grainy photographs capture mere moments of their suffering.
Shoulders drooped. Straight backed as corpses.
Crying would have required too much bodily presence.
Their eyes no longer bright. But wide. Fully wide.

Bear Paints Dirt.

White Thunder.

Cause of Death recorded in school records as *Cause of
Departure*.
Pneumonia, tuberculosis, unknown. Sometimes, *Cause of
Departure*: Death.
Disinterment for reburial in ancestral soil. These children whisper
now
among budding thickets. Dance through autumn leaves. Hum
down rain.
Giggle by waterfall. Sing across velvet canyon. Clap for jumping
fish.

Swift Bear.

Pretty Eagle.

Brave Bull.

Welcome, welcome home.

It is finally time to cry.

Virginia Watts

Someone Was Always Coughing in Donora

Monday, October 24, 1948
All was normal in Donora, Pennsylvania,
a mill town along the Monongahela River.
Coke ovens burned in the steel plant.
Stacks pumped out factory clouds
as common as sky clouds.

Tuesday
A temperature inversion dropped
a black shroud over Donora.

Wednesday and Thursday
Adults carried on in thickening, orangey air,
children rode bikes, played tag, went to school.

Friday
The lights spanning Main Street struggled and failed
to illuminate costumed children who floated by
in the Annual Halloween Parade, mere shadows.

Saturday
If you chomped, you could eat the air.
Fans at the high school football game
listened to the tackling bodies of boys
they couldn't see.

Sunday, October 30, 1948
Six thousand people sick. Fifty dead.
American Steel and Wire Works
finally shut down its smelters.
That evening, a blessing.
Rain to wash the poison away.

October 2021
Energy Transfer Company is charged with
polluting drinking water while constructing
a natural gas line across Pennsylvania.
There are two dead birds in my backyard.

What killed the birds, I do not know.
What saved me this time, my father,
his opposition to well water. I bury
the birds underneath an abandoned
Christmas tree in clay soil, beak to beak.

Virginia Watts

Keepsakes

Sixth grade girl of the 70s
riding a school bus pinching
a nickel-plated POW bracelet
tighter, tighter around her wrist
Not much else she can do
for CAPT. HUBERT WALKER JR.
Try hard not to lose him
Remember the letters of his name

That rainy morning
the bus smelled of baking bread
CAPT. HUBERT WALKER JR.
could be starving in a cell in Nam
Maybe he is a really big soldier
Maybe his dad was a Marine too
Maybe his dad calls him *Bruiser*
Maybe he can dig his way out

Sherry Eckert gets on the bus
wearing a new Flower Power bracelet
and points to my bracelet
Is your ugly bracelet gonna save him?
Sherry Eckert was born full of herself
and the world has more interesting flowers
than daises and daisies aren't psychedelic

CAPT. HUBERT WALKER JR.
was a real man in real trouble
The girl checked and
rechecked all the lists
CAPT. HUBERT WALKER JR.
didn't make it home, he sleeps
at the bottom of a ballerina jewelry box
amid smiley pins and mood rings
in the arms of a cozy, quiet attic

Capsized

On the boardwalk, a massive Viking ship ride creaks and groans. Blinks orange and red lights. Rises and falls. Builds momentum like a runaway train. I nearly scream envisioning my father among the arm-flailing passengers. All of them about to be hurled into a churning, tempestuous sea. Dad hanging on for dear life in rain-soaked khaki. A high school senior who graduated early. Enlisted. Trained to serve as a tail gunner.

The ship's captain has just spoken. *Say your prayers and goodbyes, men. This is a hurricane. Thank you for your honorable service to your country. We stand together. Be brave.* Hang on Dad, I whisper under my breath. You don't know it yet, but you're going to make it.

Watching the ride makes me nauseous. I see his body dangling between whippings at the hands of gale force winds, shredded to tatters like the sails of that ship. What if he loses his grip on the rope overtop his bunk. What if the ship rolls over, dumps him from the hull, a young, thin boy dropped like a brick into pulsing swirl, an endless tunnel drilled through the sea.

Countless times, sitting on his knee, I begged him.
*Tell me again about the storm and the ship
and how you were sure you weren't going to die.*

Virginia Watts

War Crimes

Every day, I read poems
from around the world
written contemporaneously
with Putin's invasion of Ukraine.
So many moving poems
unforgettable poems
poems of historical import.

I applaud these poets from
the comforts of my home
where my cat has a drawerful
of food and catnip treats
my clothes spin in a washer
of fragrant water
the pantry is stocked
oil tank filled to the brim
front yard fertilized green.
Enjoying this sunny day
of early spring
feels like a crime.

I finish reading
and examine
recent photos
from the war.
Wandering, one-eyed dog.
Weeping grandmother
bright yellow handkerchief
knotted under her wet chin.
Dead bodies, some children,
face down in muddy puddles,
necks bloody, frozen at broken angles.

In one photo of a mass grave
I spot robin's egg blue,
that lovely, speckled hue,
not eggs this time but the fingernails
of an ashen, slender hand breaking

though earth's surface
reaching for open air and heaven
wrist draped as if to show me
her impeccable manicure she prays
will match her Easter dress.

William Waldorf

Changeling
(exchange of infants)

Anticipation beyond completion
waits as it gathers hope it will be loved
over our present troubled position.

Like a speck of color next to a rock
catches our eye, fickle hope flirts with time.
Dressed in glamour and sparkle makes us gawk.

Afraid to trust desire's savory phantom
who like a hummingbird, darts in and out
in search for nectar, like hope for ransom.

Paid will satiate a promise fulfilled.
As if, *and*, *then* yield not to *or*, but now,
secretly hope alters, while we are thrilled.

No longer hidden, out upon a page,
my printed poem puffs me proud while on stage.

William Waldorf

War Souvenirs

They hide past deeds ashamed if you'll find them.
Children's eyes see what quiet really means
as captor's preach peace, but their actions teach
how easily they'll lose humanity.

When they fetch data from a war victim
they'll demonstrate their use of sadism.
Screams ooze out uncontrolled like muffled moans,
children frozen sit like terrified fawns.

They know death as Russian's lost empathy
will burn images into memory.
What kind of men won't raise their arms against
acts of murder done against mere infants.

Whose crime was being born from parents gone
to a grave's coffin forced to leave orphans.

William Waldorf

flowers for the trip

Light is sparse, my view tight and limited.
These accommodations now seem constrained
but can't alter or correct what's obtained
for this final ride where I'll be maintained.

All tears flow like melted snow in summer,
breaths held now struggle against their exhale.
I can feel the rumble, as feet shuffle,
as prayers are chanted for endless slumber.

Through my sunlight's warm slit there comes a noise,
surely another fellow traveler,
but eternity keeps me still with poise.
I wonder how long we'll be together.

When thumps of dirt make that fly's buzzing stop.
It must've left to find a flower shop.

William Waldorf

Green monsters

She stood in the doorway in her black dress
until she was waved to come in and sit
inside the quiet room, filled with dried flowers.
She stood straight with her gaze glued to his face
as she chose a chair near the other wife,
who bent behind with her condolences
for their newly acquired membership,
 each in their accepted dress uniform.

None discussed the green monster in the room
only how good he looks, how still, so calm,
as rage festers hidden behind their gloom.
Each thought: *not supposed to be this way,
lost her youth, but she's not distraught.*
Silence and sniff's meet fragrances' whiffs

William Waldorf

Mahsa Amini

Raised with love inside her house protected
never experienced such anger before
Naive child: its only hair she cried out
                              before being whipped in fear
   To hear,   blasphemous beast
                          respect our law.

What you wear can bring harm from many men
This is what's often heard before she died.
State's violence leaves their hubris's in bruises
on a childlike girl whose ruby shoes failed

Locked in, voices become muffled, hidden
but rise like yeast does when it finds flour
beaten down to rise again puffs up dough
to grow when heated as it proofs for truths
will ooze out unable to be contained
although their lives are often restricted
Tyrants murder all like Tiananmen square
then truth and her will never be seen here

William Waldorf

for eternity

love makes your insides burst wanting to share
    such beauty, skin softer than rose petals
    her deep flashing fiery dark eyes wrinkles
with a smile so bright, how should I compare

sunrise, sunsets seem dull, I will declare
   if one took all the worlds brightest candles
   they wouldn't equal light from those sparkles
greater than heavens' brightest moonlight stare

I love her deeply her total being
   calms me with happiness, yet in candor
when I'm away, my body is aching
   for the nearness of her, my sweet lover.

if providence ends my life abruptly
my love will remain for eternity

William Waldorf

A Nude descends

Steps echo in the circular stairwell
moonlight shimmers through an open transom
to reflect a flash of flesh, with hustle
as it descends in such fluid rhythm

an outstretched gangly limb, against the wall.
Shadows glue my view to this tormentor
whose imagined skin becomes my torture
while I wait, at the wide open portal.

Cubists paint many sides as motion flows,
they don't portray one single view of time.
While most other artists feel it's their prime
choice, different views require a new pose.

Out from the dimness of a cold stairwell
comes beauty, naked, fresh, Duchamp's bombshell.

William Waldorf

craft room voices

She talks to her love every day, she said.
From her craft room she hears him move about
the bedroom. *I think there are only four rooms.*
nightly here, they talk.

Married for more than thirty-seven years
they sit without any words spoken,
know what each is about to do next.
She prepares his meals, puts away his clothes.

He still accompanies her after his stroke
rides shotgun and warns about changing lights,
waits in the car till the market is done.
Then home to stock shelves and rock away time.

She kept the calendar the day he died
his hat hangs on a clothes rack near the door
she hung more pictures of him when he left
she won't move, here she can still talk to him.

William Waldorf

Mona Lisa thoughts

The artist painted: curiosity
overcomes beauty.
As all will ponder through eternity,
the puzzle inside this celebrity.

Realistic elusive eyes follow you.
Her calm demeanor uncomfortable.
A subtle irresistible lip curl
that seems to move with a peripheral view.

A gift from the maestro of mystery
who shadows eyebrows, but not her twinkle.
Adds wonder to her thoughts as we struggle
to perceive what they could possibly be.

Her allure stronger than the suns splendor.
All desire to know her inner treasure.

William Waldorf

Dust in the wind

One day you'll see the wonder of color
like a hunter it becomes your armor's
camouflage, but now highlights messages
of destruction. Trees become homage as
you seek solace in the forest's foliage
awash with shades from natures complexions.

Here in these glades time shares past reflections
clarifies imperfections in old age.
Each generation starts a new life phase
like trees push seeds away when each new sprout
spreads, but old growth's progress still is in doubt.

Fire claims the growth, ash becomes the mulch.
Water disappears each year. Tree growth rings
starve while ravine's moisture dries in the gulch
Without tall sentries hope like dust circles

Rodney Richards

Lips wet over mousse, red velvet, banana cream
coconut, Reese's™, tiramisu, everyone's dream
Waitress asks our choice "chocolate" we say
\ Can't wait /
She quick-like agrees, scampers away
to a radiant abundant desserts display
Our glands salivate as they anticipate
two NY-slices of deep dark satin
\ Mousse the finest /
First, sip two drinks on ice to
clean our impatient palates
\ Should be coming /
Creamy pieces appear with
mild clatters on our table.
Herald pleasure to eyes
\ Oh, oh, oh /
Wide, tall and perky
cold long wedges sit
steeped in high
foamed heaps
of whipped
whiteness
to entice,
satisfy,
slate,
o u r
Ahhs

for the factory's cheesecake

Rodney Richards

Cardinal Rules for Mates

do not disrupt your loved one's sleep
   when bartender joe calls at 2 a.m.
it doesn't help to say *I told him not to*

don't ever say *You've gained weight*
   when they say *I need new jeans*
   or you'll soon be wearing cascades
of broken dishes on your head

tread lightly when challenge their statement
   with shitty two cent opinions,unless
   your facts are invincible

their memories cannot be questioned
   do not engage or correct; listen polite-like
if argue tete-a-tete, expect a day of silence

they love you for yourself, trust in that

follow their example as your children
   learn what's right and moral

do not say *I'll get it tomorrow*
   if they say *We need milk for the cat*
put on your jacket, start the car,
drive directly to the nearest mart

do not get pissed when hear *I have a headache*
   they really do, wouldn't you?
   sex hurts self-worth when not in the mood

ask often and nice *How do you feel?*
   they'll love you more
   than a baby loves nipples
   or smothering cuddles

when they hint at a date
give a peck and jump in the shower
   pleasure is best when skin is flowered

when they forgive you, which they will
   for some god-only-knows reason
remember the pain you inflicted
   and avoid thoughtless reminders

live in the moments you love together
   they will be shorter than you'd wished for

the stage

spirit moves the souls of children
youth, women, men, every audience
  never dead, unsound, unfound,
empty of purpose, bereft of passion

no one alone in daily worldly disorder
if in sync with all-knowing playwright's inner ardor
  if ever flounder, abide director's calls for *Action!*
won't falter when velvet curtain rises to heaven

these pure and holy directors share names and titles
since Adam they swayed millions of masses
  preeminent messengers never fail to appear
and direct our gaze to the supreme composer

the play must go on to sounds of eternal music
follow your script as move from song to aria
cherish encores and second chances
only two on this stage to convince
yourself and the listening master

Rodney Richards

Can humans be fixed?

Do it now! belligerent guy tells poor concierge
he's either a blowhard or bore
invectives of hate who threatens gore
to an honest answer given, *No tickets*

I want to say %b$#d&*
to the front of his face
but hesitate
as irate asshole spits out
Don't give me excuses you liar
or I'll take my business elsewhere

and security escorts him out the door
hooray, found hotel justice today
* * *
at Acme's checkout
lowly clerk looks shaken, askance
not sure he'll appease obnoxious complaints
a simple *Yes Ma'am* does not sooth her

but manager escorts her
out the door
hooray, found grocery justice today
***
in Sheraton lobby made clear all would hear
my angry hissing
You effin' scumbag, you're in on it too,
you only carry bags for tips from the poor

apologize later
to the quiet black-haired young man
but hurts not cured, not really, not ever.
sorrowful, contrite too late
hooray, woke up to empathy that night

Rodney Richards

24/7 restaurants

Mel's Jewish deli serves hot pastrami on rye
slabs of spicy mustard, dill pickle on the side
as red-haired foxes paw reserved tables with pride

squirrels order ripe round acorns slathered
in apricot jelly and strawberry jam from Panera's
bakery halls at teen-crowded suburban malls

crunchy peanut butter smears Ritz crackers
to fill tummies of grey mice in the dead of night
as they crouch inside kitchen cabinet doors left ajar

all-night Grub Shacks welcome waddling skunks
who anticipate bowls of crawdad grasshoppers
and beetles to quell hungry nocturnal shoppers

sharp-clawed snout-nosed moles tunnel
to The Underground Trattoria for insect-covered
Sicilian pizza and sips of Red Bull® nighttime energy

all the animals guzzle their daily water from
24/7 flowing hoses next to every Friendly®'s
Dunkin'® or Wawa® storefront

if only wandering ragged homeless could find
free ready-made food and drinks instead
of being ignored and booted aside as pests

creatures tall and small try to survive
unlike way too many spoiled customers

she spoke to me

just returned from two years in  wore khakis and
Converse sneakers into junior class homeroom with strangers
named M to T

in 2nd period art class glance long at the petite mysterious girl

covered in freckles chattering, enjoying her life in the party

had been trying to make new friends and silently
    to be liked, but chummy cliques kept status quos clenched

at worktable with   when a crouched figure popped
into mind. as shape clay for 30 minutes look up in surprise.
    with no hat on, shocked by curly red hair she says,
Welcome to school, your wrestler looks cool, my name's Jan
               *   *   *

marry ourselves with no preacher outside, under brilliant June
sun in '71   she shares inner mysteries as drive to honeymoon

Rodney Richards

silver dollar senyru

look up from oak bench
smoking a fresh cigarette.
under moon's dollar

earth's shadows all black
crooked smile across my face.
same day has come back

blessed to have one more
chance to address world's deep plights.
unless piss on them

opportunities
rife to save hurting people.
lack hutzpah to do so

Get off your fat ass
Think of others needs for once.
children want to laugh

human happiness
worth forty lives to die for.
the full moon awaits

unbidden

Oh God, issues forth
  as inhale then puff,
    as stomp big black ants
      where they don't belong
robins keep chirping
    why won't they scoop down
      and eat these boring pests?

does He hear me?
    when call on Him for help
do not know
    the name He'll answer to
      so many to choose from

been waiting for Him
    to speak my name again
      as His mystic voice once did
        when thrice caught in raptures
but don't remember
    what the angels said

words can't depict ethereal floating feelings
    they created, only dreams remain
      unless i am dreaming this now
of smoke, ants and robins

Rodney Richards

on the city street at night

the shadowman chases me, running close
black wide-brimmed pointy hat
black-thick overcoat brushes his ankles
flapping in the rush
black featherweights on his hooves

his strong stick-like hand holds
a black umbrella, closed
pointed at my fleeing back
its silver-gleamed tip itches
to stab

i run harder, he behind
thump, thump, thump...
moves closer
his black arm stretches out
that damn umbrella!
ready to stab

a foot, now inches
can sense the pain
an inch, a millimeter
legs can't possibly run faster . . .
me, a man dressed in white
a slow quiet man
cannot outrun or out scream
this seven-foot warlock

a millisecond before contact
he's going to kill me!

wake cold, in a sweat
chastised for my sins
must change my ways
or he will pierce me, and then . . .

street kid polyglot

foreigners flourish since country founded
their cultures adjusted to pidgin english.
must speak ten fluid languages, more,
to maneuver around them so pickup more lingos.

italian easiest by kilometers, *caio* friendly
for hello or goodbye at corner pizza joints.
delight in forkfuls of ravioli, mostaccioli, or
fettucine al fredo and ricotta cannolis

fluent in farsi, arabic too, *insha'ullah*
mumbled when a surprising god wills it so.
allah'u'abha a mutual greeting
or muslims say *allahu 'akbar.*
respect religion or won't enter paradise

learned french in high school
can search any downtown bibliotheque.
bonjour mademoiselle before asking
voulez-vous coucher avec moi?

adopted spanish in the bordellos,
hola, me llamo valentino for the girls
with *mucho gusto* to seal the deal

shouted eff words in ten languages,
crude, universal, no need for translation.
when brought mothers into it, serious complications.
lucky my once misbehaved graduated

not shy now to open ethnic conversations,
microsoft, google, apple possess one-click
oral translators. add siri, alexa, chat ai,
and say whatever words my tongue desires

Anne Miller Christensen

I Rock

In
the arms
of Lake Sacandaga,
I rock in my granite-toned
kayak this Adirondack August
early morning. Mist hangs low over
water once quaffed by dinosaurs and
Haudenosaunee. Cohesive hydrogen and
oxygen molecules buoy me, stirred by a breeze
that began in Greenland. Pleistocene glaciers ground
down mountains over millions of years to create this silvery

"Land of the Waving Grass" lake.

Not alone, I rock.

One

Lying on a blanket this August Adirondack night,
   the Milky Way stretches overhead like another blanket.
      No jealous moon risen yet to compete, minimal light pollution.
         Ebony warm night, lulled by the language of loquacious insects.

Mute city dwellers are deprived of this
      spectacular out-of-body experience.
         Tonight's starlight has traveled across
            countless parsecs and oceans of time.

Too far to feel the furnaces of gas that live and die.
      Light from the past arrives at this moment, to this field.
         Time, space, such a small me on this star trail in this
            spinning spiral galaxy, a postage stamp of the Universe.

      I'm marked "present" tonight,
         unsure of the destination but glad for the company.

Anne Miller Christensen

First Light

Darkness at the beginning.
Nothing, a void until You kick
things off with a Big Bang.
In the swirling spiral clouds,
the Universe begins to expand.

Billions of years blink by.
Stars come and go. Earth spins,
the moon glows, continents move.
Blue-green algae, dinosaurs
and hominids evolve and die.

Abraham, Buddha, Jesus
and Mohammed try to see
Your face, teach us the
way we can peacefully live
on the Earth that we share.

Darkness then light.
Lightness of being.
Light that shines on each being.
What a good idea.
It is always about the light.

The Church of Poetry

founded in March 2020,
birthed from coronavirus
isolation and Zoom,
swings welcoming doors.
Members occupy
solitary cells, wait for
inspiration to channel
onto the page or laptop.
Quiet is our music.
We make reciprocal offerings
to each other, trust the bonds

Anne Miller Christensen

of creative celebration.
Drink sustaining support,
strive for beauty, light.

And the people say *Amen*.

Battle lines

red vs blue
sides chosen
us against them
democracy at risk
invectives hurled
alternative facts
conspiracy theories
violence—verbal, physical
deeply-felt issues
privacy rights denied
racial injustice
economic disparity
mass shootings
"dark" money
campaign ad saturation
rolls purged
early, mail-in, day-of votes
suppressed
gerrymandered
no Souls to the Poll
long lines, a crime to give water
drop box intimidation
poll workers threatened
election results denied

more
"We the People"
please

Anne Miller Christensen

The Sacred Space

A sacred blooming,
flower-filled garden

I blissfully levitate, buzzing
with industrial-strength happiness

Consumed in communion with
periwinkle stars, petunia-scented kisses

Be they tulips, cherry blossoms, orchids,
irises, roses, wildflowers or morning glories

Serotonin, dopamine, oxytocin and endorphins run
rampant when surrounded by nature's sacred bower

But how to deal with the thorny
short span of such Eden beauty?

Substitute stolen photographic
memory-scrolls of this joy

The maintenance rainy-day fund,
until Paradise is regained

Waxed Amaryllis

Christmas
a waxed bulb arrives
nestled in an Amazon box
cropped leaves expectant
despite challenging year
scary epidemiology

draws on moisture
energy stored in bulb
like inner reserves
we will mine
to grow
into new year

Anne Miller Christensen

Psalm 151
Prayer of a weary world

We are broken, truly
broken. A shredded
world, justice dried
up. Mercy disappears.

Children do not survive to
praise You. Mothers weep
while Fathers despair. The
greedy prosper and thrive.

An overheated world battles
for water, food, vaccines.
The poor struggle to survive,
as the rich push them aside.

War and conflict break out.
Tribal hatred destroys love.
Division grows, understanding
evaporates. Refugees flee.

Hope dies in the womb.
Our night is long, the
dawn too far from us.
Where is deliverance?

Right the wrongs of this world.
Rescue the children who long
for You, our only true hope. Heal
and free all the brokenhearted.

Lord, make haste. Change the
hard hearts of those who have
turned from the ways of goodness.
We trust Your great care will prevail.

Anne Miller Christensen

Embroidery in the time of pandemic

Satin stitch, fishbone, split,
French knot, together we
bend over our floral embroidery,
a refuge to forget the virus.

Despite early pandemic days,
stretched linen in a hoop
opens a welcome window with
a NY Botanical Garden Zoom class.

Limited floss colors ordered online
but delivered on time; could have
used more shades of green.
YouTube tutorials studied, replayed.

Unbroken creative chain through the ages,
captures beauty, sweetens darkness.
Stitch by stitch, blooms record time,
beauty for today, tomorrow.

Awake

    driving home
        on autopilot

            golden sunset, ink black clouds
            awaken attention

                spotlighted autumn leaves
                glow in fading glory

                    I drive, enveloped
                      by setting spotlight

                          unexpected, brief gifts
                          GPS the moment

Anne Miller Christensen

With Utter Joy

With utter joy
a racing river otter
belly flops,
slips and slides
in a ribbon of water
at the Central Park Zoo.
Joy upon joy.
You and your young son
stroll in the spring sunshine,
drinking in the song
of nature…life.
A glow surrounds you both.
You hurry to hear the half hour
chiming of the Delacorte clock.
See two monkeys hammer the bell,
while a mechanical menagerie of
bear
penguin
goat
kangaroo
hippo
and
elephant
rotate and play nursery rhymes.
You want to freeze
this place
and this time
for this child,
fashion a fairy tale
with hearty helpings
of happiness.
But you move on
to the adorable puffins,
fitted in formal wear
with clown-bill accents,
parenting their pufflings,
swimming stories filled
with fishes and serene seas

Anne Miller Christensen

Poem of Recommendation

I speak for one today
(rather, two)
the caterpillar and butterfly

there is much
to recommend
the former,
a vegetarian
who munches
with purpose,
while the latter
wafts on wind

but between the two,
a chrysalis stage
hides the magic
of reconstitution
and transformation

one could do worse
than inhabit
a terrestrial
and subsequent
aerial lifestyle,
with a stopover
in Nature's
changing room

Anne Miller Christensen

The Book Club

City kids set to read
Charlotte's Web.
What is friendship
in the country, in the
city, in a pandemic?

Can Charlotte, a blood-thirsty spider,
really be friends with Wilbur,
a poor pig prone to fainting when
the going gets tough?

Loneliness eats away
at the young pig, at us.
Yet Wilbur harbors doubts
about this arachnid.

When Wilbur wails that he is eating
to become the Christmas meal,
Charlotte promises to save him.

Charlotte is a writer. She weaves
words into her web: *some pig*, *terrific*,
radiant (a prompt from a soap suds ad)
and, finally, the topper—*humble*.
All these words to describe
her dear friend, Wilbur.

I'll ask the kids
for words that describe
their friends.

One of the mothers
tells me her son
cried when Charlotte died.

I am not sure how to
handle that part.
We'll have to talk.

Anne Miller Christensen

My Dream

asleep in my bed
eyes shut tight against
current cruel catastrophes

I weave a world
I want to hug
close to my heart

there is no more
red and blue
in the paintbox

purple is the color
of choice, harmony
the measure of music

out of an abundance
of love, we agree
to vaccinate

no more to mutate
masks are not required
but we desire

to protect to guard
the safety of all
regardless of color

voter registration drives
collect
the will of the people

toxic social media
disappears
due to disinterest

I don't want
to wake.

Joan Menapace

Red Wagon

It needed weekly maintenance
for at least one squeaky wheel.
Mom used an oilcan, the one

with the long spout that
made a guck-guck sound
when you pressed the bottom.

I always whined to do it
oily fingers, oil spills.
Mom had to do cleanup, again.

The Radio Flyer wagon had solid
rubber wheels
small and black which

gradually wore down.
Rough pocked
pits made by the gravel

paths we clumbered on our way
to the unfarmed fields where the
bugs and birds were.

The steel wagon had a wooden
three-sided slated panel
that supported the back of

big sis who supported mine.
Matching leather closed-toe sandals on
legs straight out bounced

to the rhythm of the hard
wagon bed while plucky Mom
pulled the long black metal handle

Joan Menapace

the three of us in
matching blue shorts, red and white
horizontal striped shirts

not patriotic on purpose.

Joan Menapace

Allie

I think of you at breakfast in the morning
when I cut my boiled egg in half.
It lasts twice as long to eat that way
      you say.

I think of you at lunchtime
while chopping cucumbers and leftover chicken.
Crisp salad most reminds me of you in LA
      everyday.

I think of you when I mix my five-o-clock
perfect manhattan because
you say *you drink too much,*
      by the way.

I think of you after dinner now
      wonder about forced solitude and you
      worry about danger near to you
      wanting you closer, me and you
      wish to have adventures again

      like the times you used to sit sturdy
      on the handlebar face forward
      arms straight, knees up, dirty from street play
      feet on the vintage balloon-tire fender,
      biking up spruce street
      both sweaty
      to cool off in the art museum's fountains.
      Hold tight now.
      I'd puff in your little left ear.

jubilation

you know it when it happens
the bubbly feeling
you are over-stimulated by

so many beautiful choices
food says go away from me
even sex has slipped to second place

your brain space is twittering with possibilities
the devil on your other shoulder left town
free to make unilateral decisions

you laugh and possibly dance your joy.
you can drink your pleasure in sloppy gulps
burp without pardon

your excitement is uncontainable
reason and critical thinking take a long nap.
love walks in the door and stays

stays
strong as long as you choose

Joan Menapace

Over-stimulated

Outside the small wooden grey house
cradled on two sides by
experienced rhododendrons

now in temporal bloom
the air around me teems with
energy bits that jiggle my head.

The sounds of mid-May glisten
with greens growing
if you listen. Louder

in comparison to two weeks ago.
The smell of life outside the hospital
rumples my brain with gratitude.

So much entertainment in a small moment.
I'm home now
I need to get back inside.

Joan Menapace

Preparations

I wonder if I'll live long enough
to get myself ready to die?

Better start sorting through my secrets
keep only the juicy ones.

Stash regrets in plastic storage tubs
I might not want to lose any.

Toss unkept promises into the compost
hope they will rot quickly.

Will I be able to access
recent mistakes in the Cloud?
I've forgotten already who to forgive.

Fear, anxiety and hopelessness
go in the burn pile. Fire away.

But love,
tell me dear,
if I start storing it now
will it still be good
after its expiration date?

Joan Menapace

out walking: thoughts

escorting
our old dog
each night was his idea
left on her own
the little thing
bark scared
now he walks alone
headlamp as companion
he paces his perimeter path
and sorts thoughts
in his private deck
dealing them one at a time
like solitaire cards
playing themselves out

shuffle redeal
shuffle
redeal

Joan Menapace

the blue hour

after mauve skies
comes l'heure bleu
the Norway spruce stands
the tallest tree nearby
sways slow   limbering

he welcomes her magic
blueness into his
viridian hammock
she envelopes his bough
until moist darkness clings
to them
like frothy soup
slow and long
simmered   blended
together

it's nutty odor
attracts dawn's
ready nose

l'heure bleu flees
a vaporous whirr

he trembles in secret

Joan Menapace

The Mist & the Meadow

The hill across the valley
wakes and sees
pink mist below. It thinks,

*she doesn't blush like that
everyday.* Her gossamer
skirt spreads wide, sly,

settling on the fragile tops
of the strawgrass.
Stalks vibrate. Seeds

spray the meadow, reflect
a flash of rose back
to the transfixed

hill's eyes. Dainty
mist tickles for
a few seconds until

the hot sun dissipates
the quivering. I rise
nonchalant, look outside

hear a susurrus of an
echo throughout
the valley. Can a hill
sigh?

Joan Menapace

The Perennial Quarrel

He, troublemaker Autumn,
uses Equinox Wind
to blow up
sister Summer's languid blanket,
doesn't know how she could just lie
around and sweat and smell.
Little brother Breeze fans her
permeating bouquet. She sighs, raises her
arms overhead and spreads her
verdant stink. It is that time of year.

Like an impatient bull,
head low, Equinox Wind
circles one time then charges.

His first pass spreads cinders
in her eyes and dust in
her mouth. Summer doesn't
like that at all.
Like every brother and sister
she thunders the last word,
rises up
spits shakes mutters
angry

her lightening sword
slits the horizon
over and over

BOOM!

Toads squeeze into holes
fish still mid-swim
horses paw the sky
dogs jump into bathtubs,
hide under beds, low tables
who knows where birds go.

Joan Menapace

BOOMBOOM!

Kids pull up the covers
tea kettles pop lids
papers slide off desks
back doors whip open
hinges snap
while brother Autumn chases sister Summer.

She turns, fights back,
retreats,
repeats,
slam-bam,
a two-day spat
until bored
she storms southward,
splashes into the Caribbean Sea
her consolation bath.

As usual she bequeaths
the annual rivalry crown
to her brother,
nonchalant   cocksure   cold.

Shriveled twigs click applause.
Autumn bows.   Victory.

Joan Menapace

Inspired by Grace Paley's poem, *I Went Out Walking*

the woods are crowded with poets
this time of year
a guy carries his notebook
across his chest like a schoolgirl
his pen rides on the tip of his ear
latest poem safe in his arms

a woman head down reads a
black sketchbook an inch from her nose
a child holds on to her pen
pulls her out of the way
of the poet incoming at ten o'clock
whose stride belies the fact that the folder
in her right hand is heavy
with her first hundred poems

where paths cross two guys,
both of a certain age
stop to swap poems
so they could read them
in another voice
further along a woman
picks up scraps
which slip from
her briefcase of poems
spilling felt tip pens whenever she bent over

in the distance, in the high straw grass,
too many to count,
poets stride with purpose
like young lions across the savannah
tawny hair tangled with distraction
lovingly walk their poems
out for a breath of fresh air

Poet Bios

Nancy Cathers Demme, author of the *The Ride* (2019), a novel, has had her poetry and short stories published in *Confrontation*, Los Galesburg's *Weekend Excerpts*, *The Kelsey Review*, *US1*, the *Foliate Oak Literary Magazine*, *Willard & Maple*, *Paterson Literary Review* and *US1 Worksheets*.

She was nominated for the Pushcart Prize by *The Kelsey Review*.

Nancy has facilitated the Twin Rivers Writers' Group for 30 years and teaches *Writing in English* for ESL students. She is also an active member of the Garden State Storytellers League.

elliot m rubin is a novelist and poet who has appeared in numerous anthologies, won poetry contests, and published over thirty books of poetry.

Over ten thousand poets follow him on Instagram at elliot_m_rubin, and his crime novels have four and five-star reviews on Amazon Books.

He has also been published in many Orthodox Jewish magazines and has written two books of Jewish humor.

His website is www.CreativeFiction.net

Virginia Watts is the author of poetry and stories found in

CRAFT, *The Florida Review, Reed Magazine, Pithead Chapel, Permafrost Magazine,* and *Broadkill Review* among others.

Her poetry chapbooks are available from Moonstone Press.

She has been nominated four times for a Pushcart Prize and Best of the Net.

A short story collection is upcoming from The Devil's Party Press.

Visit her at https://virginiawatts.com/

William Waldorf (Bill) and his love affair with poetry began

with strict forms like sonnets.

Currently, he is focused on poems from daily life. He loves to show history has not changed us.

His 153 page book, *Sonnets and More,* explores various themes of love relationships.

A new book of poems is expected to be published in 2023. Bill's work has also been highlighted in *The Thursday Poets' Anthology.*

Rodney Richards (Rod) has authored two volumes of 100 topical essays each, also published individually online at bahaiteaching.org and on Instagram.

He published his rollercoaster memoir *Coffee, Cigarettes, Death & Mania* in 2022. Rod's poems have been published in *The Drunken Llama* and *The Thursday Poets' Anthology.* The Kelsey Review published his short story *Bike Slide.*

He's guided the Hamilton Creative Writers since 2012. His company ABLiA Media helps writers edit, polish, and publish their works. Contact 1950ablia@gmail.com or visit https://www.rodneyrichards.info

Anne Miller Christensen, wading in the shallow end of the pool of poetics, graduated from haiku to longer works during the pandemic.

A fan of the Emily Dickinson school of publishing, she celebrated her first published poem last year in *US 1 Worksheets.*

Warm nurturing from the Zoom Osher Lifelong Learning Institute, Rutgers University (OLLI-RU) classes and Chautauqua Institution workshops, as well as spin-off groups, have helped in the creation of the poems in this anthology. Thank you for reading.

Joan Menapace is a visual artist who has been writing poems  over the years in response to thoughts and ideas she is less able to communicate in any other form.

She views poems as word collages. Putting words together to form an image for the reader, she believes, is much like selecting marks, colors and other media to create a visual artwork.

She published her first chapbook, *WALKING* in 2022. Her website is joanmenapace.com.

Special thanks to Joan and Rodney for their efforts and time spent putting this anthology together.

In closing . . .

To all poetry lovers and
patrons, thank you from
all of us. The world is a
better place when poets
express their hearts, minds,
and feelings.

Poetry is painting that speaks.
                    Plutarch

Made in the USA
Middletown, DE
04 April 2023

27701224R10056